Christmas Wombat

written by
Jackie French

illustrated by
Bruce Whatley

Angus&Robertson
An imprint of HarperCollins*Children's Books*

Angus&Robertson
An imprint of HarperCollins*Children'sBooks*, Australia

First published in Australia in 2011
by HarperCollins*Publishers* Australia Pty Limited
ABN 36 009 913 517
harpercollins.com.au

HarperCollins*Publishers*
Level 13, 201 Elizabeth Street, Sydney, NSW 2000, Australia
Unit D1, 63 Apollo Drive, Rosedale, Auckland 0632, New Zealand
A 53, Sector 57, Noida, UP, India
1 London Bridge Street, London SE1 9GF, United Kingdom
2 Bloor Street East, 20th Floor, Toronto, Ontario M4W 1AA, Canada
195 Broadway, New York NY 10007, USA

National Library of Australia Cataloguing-in-Publication data:

French, Jackie.
    Christmas Wombat / Jackie French ; illustrator: Bruce Whatley.
    ISBN: 978 0 7322 9171 6 (hbk.)
    ISBN: 978 0 7322 9172 3 (pbk.)
    For pre-school age.
    Wombats—Juvenile fiction, Christmas stories.
    Whatley, Bruce.
A823.3

Bruce Whatley used acrylic paints on watercolour paper to create the illustrations for this book
Original cover and internal design by Priscilla Nielsen; based on design by HarperCollins Design Studio
Colour reproduction by Graphic Print Group, Adelaide, South Australia
Printed by RR Donnelley in China, on 128gsm Matt Art

14 13 12 11   16 17 18 19

To Beth, with love and wombats.
JF

For Lana, Lincoln and Harry — Merry Christmas.
BW

Slept.

Scratched.

Slept.

Ate grass.

Dangly things bumped
against my nose!

Got rid of them.

Smelled **carrots!**

Strange creatures are eating MY carrots!

Fought major battle
with strange creatures!

Won the battle.

Feeling tired.

Found the perfect spot
to have a nap.

I smell carrots!

Strange creatures trying to eat my carrots!

Got rid of them.
Again.

Carrots delicious.

Off to find **more** carrots.

A wombat hole?

Carrots!

Not easy to
get back up.

Scratched.

Have misjudged strange creatures. They can be useful for finding carrots.

Never knew there were so many carrots in the world!

Carrots!

Carrots!

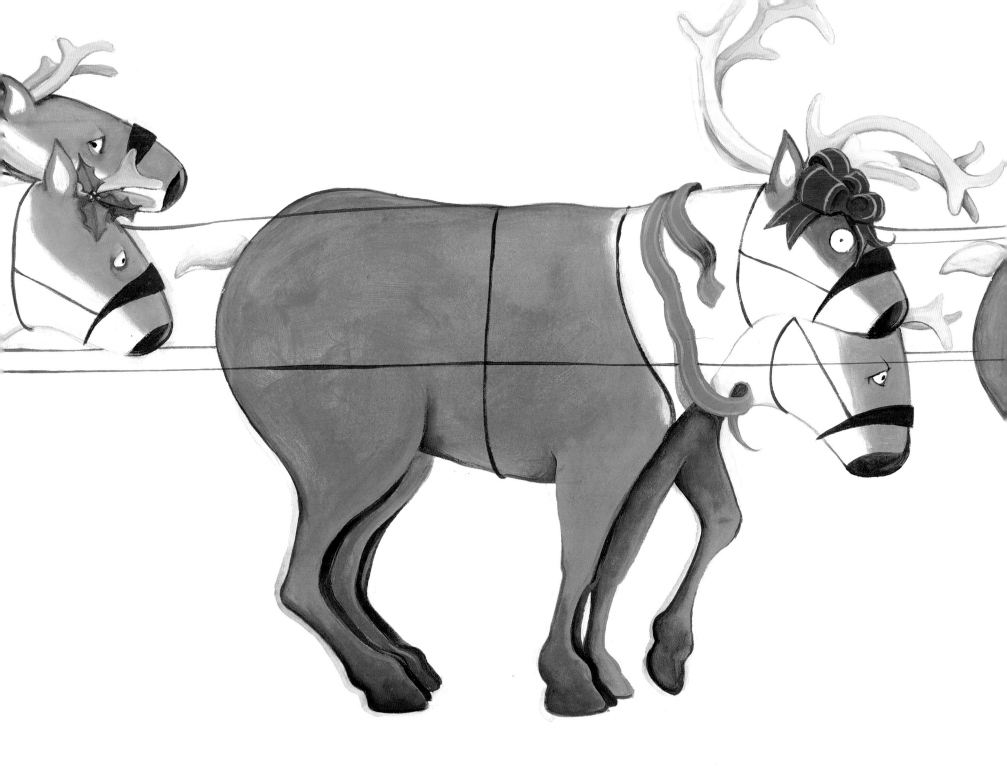

Said goodbye to
strange creatures.
Hope they visit
again soon!

Grass delicious ... but for some reason not hungry.

Slept.